W9-BHO-292

First edition for the United States, Canada, and the Philippines
published in 1989 by Barron's Educational Series, Inc.

First published by Piccadilly Press Limited, London, England.

All inquiries should be addressed to:
Barron's Educational Series, Inc.
250 Wireless Boulevard
Hauppauge, NY 11788

International Standard Book No. 0-8120-6133-0
Library of Congress Catalog Card No. 89-6482

Library of Congress Cataloging-in-Publication Data

Maddox, Tony.
Spike, the sparrow who couldn't sing
text and illustrations
by Tony Maddox.
p. cm.
Summary: With the help of Wise Old Owl, Spike the sparrow tries
to find somebody who can teach him to sing. His search brings
surprising results.
ISBN 0-8120-6133-0
(1. Birds – Fiction. 2. Animals – Fiction.) I. Title.
PZ7.M25647Sp 1989
(E) – dc19

89-6482
CIP
AC

PRINTED IN GREAT BRITAIN
9012 9697 987654321

SPIKE

The Sparrow Who Couldn't Sing!

Text and Illustrations by
Tony Maddox

New York · Toronto

Spike the Sparrow
didn't know how to sing!

When he tried, the other birds
covered their ears so they couldn't hear.

This made Spike so unhappy that
he simply stopped trying.

Sadly, he wandered off alone.

When he came to the Hollow Tree, he
heard his friend, Wise Old Owl, say,
"Cheer up, Spike, things can't be that bad."

"I just don't know how to sing,"
replied Spike with a sigh.
"Then," said Wise Old Owl, wisely,
"We will have to find someone
to show you how."

Off they went to find Mrs. Cow. Wise Old Owl explained that Spike needed someone to show him how to sing.

"When I sing," said Mrs. Cow,
"all I do is go Moooo! Moooo!"
So Spike tried, "Craawk! Craawk!"
It sounded awful!

The next animal they met
was Freddie the Fieldmouse.
"Can you show Spike how to sing?"
asked Wise Old Owl.

"Certainly," said Freddie.
"Just go Squeak! Squeak! Squeak!"
This time, Spike tried very hard and went,
"Craaawk! Craaawk! Craaawk!"
which sounded even worse than before.

When they came to the pond, they saw Mother Duck with her family of ducklings.

“Can you sing?” called Wise Old Owl.

"Of course we can!" replied Mother Duck, and all the ducklings splashed their feet and went . . .

"Quack" "Quack"

"It's no use,"
said Spike tearfully.
"I'll never be able to sing."

"Don't give up,"
said Wise Old Owl.
"Why not stay here and practice
all by yourself?"

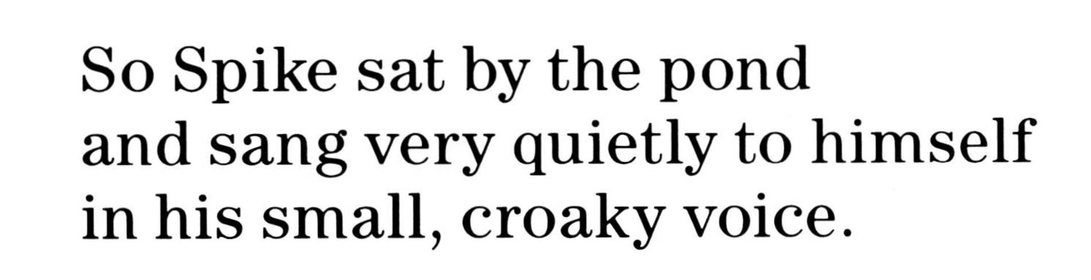

So Spike sat by the pond
and sang very quietly to himself
in his small, croaky voice.

And then he noticed
a large Green Frog
sitting on a lily pad.

"I was admiring your voice,"
said Green Frog.
"Perhaps we could sing together?"
"But all I do is croak," said Spike.
"I know," replied Green Frog.
"It sounds quite wonderful!"

Together they sang
in their croaky voices.

It wasn't long before other Frogs came and joined in.

"This is fun," thought Spike happily.
"I can sing!" he cried out loud.
"I REALLY CAN SING!"

And all the Frogs agreed!